Fever Dreams

Dev Solovey

UNVEILING NIGHTMARES PRESS

For the kids whose teachers called them "difficult" in school.

Content Warnings

Transphobia, gore, substance abuse, mental illness, animal cruelty, child abuse, trauma

CONTENTS

CYCLE 0

Smoke curls into my nostrils, stinging sweetly, as if flowers could bite. Through my half-sleeping haze, I recognize the smell—it's dragon's blood incense, the kind Masha likes to burn. I crack my eyes open. Next to my head is a black votive candle, placed on a circle of salt and ash that stretches out around me. I hear voices—one is my sister's, but I don't recognize the other. It's low and guttural, like a wolf mimicking human speech. I try to sit up and look around.

I can't move.

I hear footsteps, and then two bare feet with black painted toenails stop in front of my head. The figure squats down, and I see that it's Masha, brushing back her silky red hair. She's wearing the same pink plaid pajamas she always wears during the winter, underneath an apron covered in red stains which I can only hope are paint. In her hand is a black object with a single silver dot at the top. No, a steel rivet, in a black handle. With a blade at the other end.

"Apparently the dose I gave you wasn't enough."

Her serene smile makes the confession that she's drugged me all the more gut-twisting. I glare at her. I barely tolerate Masha. The doctors who like to slap labels on everything say she has antisocial personality disorder, but so do I, and I'm not the reason our family had to stop buying new pets. My sister is a psychopath, plain and simple, and I'm not afraid to tell her. I try to do so right now, but all that comes out is a faint groan.

"I would give you more, if there were any left in Mom's stash," Masha says. "I'm not too worried about it though." She adjusts the knife in her hand, a glimmer of grim delight in her eyes. "At least this way, I get to see what you look like when you feel it."

I try to swing at her, to shout some kind of insult, but all I can do is twitch and wheeze.

"Oh, sh-sh-shh," Masha says, putting a finger to my lips. "It won't last longer than a few minutes."

A switch flips on in my head. I'm a deer on an opiate highway, and the glint of candlelight reflecting off her blade is a pair of headlights speeding towards me. The truth, that Masha is going to murder me, finally sets in. If I don't do something, I'm going to die.

Blinding pain ripples out from the left side of my stomach, the cold metal slicing through my flesh and exposing my organs. The stroke is slow and calculated, making it all the worse. A sound that should have been a scream escapes my leaden lungs. Finally my tongue moves, and I wheeze, "stop..."

"The ritual ends when your blood runs cold," Masha replies sweetly. "Don't worry, I haven't cut any important arteries yet." Her frigid fingers gently lift my shirt higher. "You'll be alive for most of it, in fact."

The tip of her knife punctures my abdomen again, just below my diaphragm. A white-hot streak of pain follows it. "Stop," I say again, louder this time.

"You'll experience so many new sensations," Masha says, ignoring me. "Pleasure and pain, burning and freezing, choking and drowning." Another stroke of her knife, and she pulls open my skin, exposing the contents of my stomach. She fingers my intestines.

I make a noise approaching a scream. I have to call for help. We have neighbors, I know they should hear me. I just have to be louder. I try again, the volume of my voice barely increasing.

Masha continues her rambling as she pushes my organs around. "Euphoria that only the most radiant of gods can feel, despair beyond all mortal suffering." As she speaks, her voice drops lower and lower, morphing into an inhuman growl. "Such angelic agony, washed in sparkling rivers of tears and blood." I finally manage to move my head, and she notices, staring back at me with black eyes. Her face starts to melt, revealing the blood and bone beneath it. "Oh, how I envy you, Thaddeus..."

Finally, I scream. I scream for help, again and again, hoping someone will hear—my parents, my neighbors, anyone. She finally clips an artery, and the blood rushes out of me in throbbing waves, taking my consciousness with it.

Cycle 1

The chirping wakes me from my nightmare. I groan and pull a pillow over my head. A while ago, I might have been thankful to the bird for waking me from that dream, but after hearing its ranting every morning for a while now, I'm just tired of it.

Unable to get back to sleep, I toss the pillow to the side, yawn and rub my eyes, then check my phone. Most of the notifications are from Discord servers I keep forgetting to mute, but I eventually find one from my friend Matthias.

mayhematthias 01/06/2022 3:44 AM
```
the cookies gave me arsenic poison-
ing
```

I narrow my eyes. No, that's not what it says.

mayhematthias 01/06/2022 3:40 PM

```
the cook gave me poisoning arsenic
```

Another message pops up. I have to squint in order to read it.

mayhatthiasma 31/6/22022 3:40 MM

```
cook arsenc in the poison the
Ijk ESPN? they threw thre me out of
a boat
```

It takes me three tries to read it, and the words shift every time. As I struggle to piece together a response, more messages flood in.

myhathiasmahe 00/00/528491 6:oo0 MS

```
arsenc in the poison the cookie
sfsn ASDF? thROW YOURSELF out of a
boat succumb
happinees is submission
stpo living
```

I attempt to reply.

> matthis what th fuck are y tlkingg abot|

I feel like I can't control my thumbs. I try again.

> matthsa why are re you sa|

I grind my teeth. The moment I fix one typo, another appears, and I feel like my words are changing as I type them.

matthsa why i will ujmp off cliff submit to hte |

That's not even what I wanted to say. I look back up at his messages, only to find they've been reduced to glyphs and symbols. I try again and again, and before long I don't even remember how I wanted to respond, or even what I was responding to in the first place. Every time I start to type a sentence, it morphs into a completely different one halfway through.

I decide that replying to messages while I'm still half asleep isn't a good idea. I set my phone down and sit up, putting on the ratty green Baja sweater that I've had since I was thirteen.

More memories of the nightmare come to me. Vivid dreams are a side effect of the antipsychotics I take, but I've never felt such intense pain in one before—at least, not enough to remember it. I can still feel the cold metal of the blade gliding through my flesh, like scissors through wrapping paper. My chest tightens with anxiety.

This is hardly the first time I've dreamed about my sister killing me. For as long as I can remember, she has always taken things too far—even when we were kids, she would rationalize gore and abuse into our play. Using our toy kitchen set turned into pretend cannibalism, cops and robbers devolved into the Stanford prison experiment. If I ever told our parents, she would always find some way to spin the story and make it sound like I started it. Her current obsession with the occult is only a continuation of her violent tendencies.

I finally feel warm enough to get out of bed, and I swing my legs over the side, stepping into my faded Pikachu slippers. I check my phone again and try rereading Matthias's message. When I open discord, I frown, staring at the screen. This isn't the conversation I remember. Now that I think about it, I can't remember what the conversation was about at all. I try to respond, but once again, the text keeps shifting, and I struggle to type my answer. For a brief moment, it occurs to me I might be dreaming still.

I look at my blanket. It's the same dry, lint-covered comforter I've had since childhood, complete with printed patterns of SpongeBob characters. I run my fingers over the surface, and I can feel the bump of each ball of lint beneath them. I go to my dresser and pull out the cologne my Baba bought me last year, to commemorate me starting HRT. The memory makes me smile. I spray a bit on my wrist, then smell it. The tobacco-vanilla scent is as potent as I remember.

Every sensory detail is clear to me. I can smell the cologne, feel the cool bottle in my hands. I can sense the weight of my own body, the indents of the lumpy weaved rug pressing into the bottom of my slippers, the cold air entering my lungs with each breath. No, I'm not dreaming. Why can't I read what's on my phone?

I close my eyes and turn towards my small bookshelf. I don't remember the order of every single book I own, but I do remember the first few on the top shelf—*Pride and Prejudice, Alice in Wonderland, The Book Thief, Hogfather, Coraline*. I open my eyes. They're sitting on the shelf as always, in that same order. I open *Pride and Prejudice* and read the first sentence. "It is a universal truth that a single man with a good fortune must—" No, it's changing. Now it reads, "It is a truth universally acknowledged that a single man in possession of fortune, should—" I close my eyes again. I don't remember the exact words. Perhaps the book in my hands can't remember them either.

I shut the book.

I'm no stranger to madness. I've been in psychosis enough times that I developed a system for figuring out how far gone I am—granted, if I'm too far gone, I won't be lucid enough to remember my system, but at the moment, I can still think. I run through a mental checklist:

1. Can I still think rationally? Yes.

Proof: I just used reasoning to test a hypothesis.

2. Am I manic? No.

Proof: I'm not jittery enough.

3. Am I anxious? Yes.

Is there a cause? Yes, I can't seem to read anything without the words changing.

Would another reasonable person be anxious in this situation? Yes.

Is it therefore affecting my judgment? No.

Proof: See item #1.

4. Am I depressed? No.

Proof: I got out of bed.

5. Did I get enough sleep? Probably not.

Is it affecting my cognition? No.

Proof: See item #1.

6. Am I hearing anything? Yes.

What am I hearing? A bird chirping.

Is the bird real?

I put the book back on the shelf and plug my ears. I still hear the chirping, but it's muffled, which means the sound probably isn't coming from inside my head. Just to be sure, I look out my window. After craning my neck for a minute or so, I finally see the nest on a branch a few feet to the left of my bedroom window. A little brown sparrow perches next to it, yapping its head off.

So, I'm not experiencing auditory hallucinations. Those usually come before any other psychotic symptoms, which means I'm not at the point where I should be getting visual ones. And yet, here I am, seeing unreadable text.

A theory takes form in my head, as well as another idea to test it. I open one of the plastic drawers of art supplies in my closet and take out my box of Prismacolor markers. Before opening it, I try to remember the order of colors. I can recall the first three on the top row (forest green, tuscan red, turquoise), the location of the black marker (last one on the bottom row), and the order of the blue, yellow, orange and purple markers. (I know they're in that order in the bottom row, but I don't remember exactly where the sequence starts.) The plastic latch pops open, and I pull off the top, examining the markers. The forest green, tuscan red, turquoise, and black markers are all where I expect them to be, but the other colors keep changing and shifting, most of them indistinct. I eventually find the sequence of blue, yellow, orange and purple, but the blue keeps shifting along the bottom row, pulling the other three colors with it.

I look up at the clothes in my closet, and it's more of the same—my jacket is where I always keep it, but the rest of the clothes keep changing places. My shoes all look like boots, sandals, and sneakers, all at once. Trying to discern the details of my reality feels like trying to focus a camera on an object that's constantly moving. The only things I can really see, it seems, are the things that I remember clearly, and I can only see them in as much detail as is present in my memory.

Or at least, that's the case with most of the stuff in here. The only exception is the sparrow. I recognize the chirping, but until today I was always too annoyed to actually go looking for its nest. I had never seen the bird itself before. There's no way I could have known what it looked like. But unlike any of the other things I can't remember well enough, the sparrow is distinct.

At this point in my life, I've learned that going to the hospital with this sort of thing really only has a twenty percent chance of doing me any good. Most of the time when I seek help, they either downplay a serious crisis, or admit me into the psych ward for trivial reasons. The medical system isn't without its uses, but really, finding stability is easiest when I'm in control of what's happening to me. Right now, I have control, and I am determined to keep it that way.

I decide to go about my day normally until I find a solution, starting with a pot of fresh coffee. I pull my sweater tighter around me, then walk over to my door and turn the handle.

The moment I step through, the floor drops out from under me.

The sensation of falling, like my soul escaping my body, grips me as I hurtle face-first through the clouds and plummet into the Chicago skyline. I scream at first, but the wind blasting past my face makes it impossible to inhale. The change in air pressure and mounting velocity nearly rip my eardrums out of my head, and soon all I can hear is ringing.

My body begins to twist and cramp as it burns through the last few molecules of oxygen in my blood. As my vision darkens, I feel something grab the back of my collar. Something with talons.

CYCLE 2

I jolt awake. Again, the bird is chirping. I look outside my window, and I can still see it—a rust colored sparrow, babbling away.

E verything else is upside down.

I still feel like I'm right side up, and I think I am. But every item in my home has been flipped on its head, in many cases defying the laws of physics. My desk is somehow balancing on the pencils in my pencil jar, and despite one of the drawers being slightly open, nothing is falling out of it. I still feel like I'm lying on my mattress, but when I look down, I realize I'm on top of the slats on the underside of my bed frame.

Strangely, I can remember my nightmare with perfect clarity. The items in my home shifting and changing, the unreadable text, falling out of the sky. It doesn't come to me in bits and pieces, the way dreams usually do. I remember it as if it really happened. I also remember the one before it, as much as I wish I didn't. I can still feel Masha's fingers rooting around inside my guts.

I look out the window. The tree is upside-down, its dirt-caked roots reaching into the air. After a minute or so, I finally spot the bird's nest—upside-down again, having somehow not fallen out of its place on the branch. The bird is perched on what is now the underside of its nest, yelling its little lungs out. But just like me, it's still right-side up.

I decide I've had enough of this mess, and I need to go to the hospital. Sure, they fumble their job more often than not, but if this really is some new flavor of psychosis, a doctor will know more about it than I do.

I get out of bed and attempt to put my clothes on, although I have to go down to the floor to look under my drawers, just so I can see what's in them. When I finally pull out an outfit, I try to put it on, only to find that each item wants to be upside down no matter how many times I rotate it. The same happens when I try to put on my shoes. Unable to dress myself, I give up and decide to stay in my pajamas. I fumble with the drawers on my bedside table until finally pulling out my bus pass, then head for the door. Whatever this is, I want it to end as soon as possible.

The moment I open the door, I'm stumbling into the woods. The strange effect of everything being upside down hasn't gone away—all the pine trees are balancing on the needles of what should have been the very top, with their roots curling up into the sky. My momentum takes me forward before I can stop myself. I whip around to go back inside, but the door slams shut before me. When I open it, there's nothing behind it but more trees. A single door in the middle of a forest, was completely useless to me.

Stranded in the woods with nothing but my pajamas, I have no choice but to walk. The more I look at my surroundings, the more disorienting the upside-down effect becomes. Every rock is upturned, and every shrub is suspended by the tips of its tallest branches—even the squirrels that pass by are somehow running on their heads. I see a colony of ants near a boulder, and when I look closer, I find they're all upside down, marching along with their legs stuck in the air.

The hair on the back of my neck stands on end, and an uneasy sensation creeps up my spine. I feel a hundred invisible eyes on me, a sensation I recognize. In my moments of crisis, when my brain is all chaos, and everything seems real, even the things that aren't, this is always the first thing I feel—like I'm not alone.

I don't usually ascribe to spiritual stuff. I have to actively avoid it, as accepting the existence of the supernatural could lead to me eventually endorsing delusions, and I can't open myself up to that possibility. But in my soul, in my marrow, I know there are things I can't explain. There's something beyond the mortal and tangible, something awful that lies just under the boundaries of reality. A sinking feeling in my gut tells me I'm having a brush with it.

A low vibration ripples the air, rumbling through my chest and radiating outward. The sound envelops my organs, wracking me with a wave of nausea. I hear footsteps behind me, and I whirl around with clenched fists.

A massive white stag stands in the middle of the path before me, right-side up. Wisps of light coil around it, and small gusts of airbrush the leaves beneath its hooves away. The beams of its antlers extend around its head like a halo of thorns, with five points on either side, all of them deadly sharp. I feel it looking at me, but it has no eyes—only empty sockets where its eyes should be. It's beautiful, but with the aura of a curse. Something about this stag is an omen of disaster.

Slowly, it turns its head to face me. The vibrations swell, rattling my insides with a torrential interference of frequencies. As I stare at the creature, dread crawling along my skin, I realize it's not lacking eyes at all. In fact, it has a surplus of them—one on each tip of its antlers, blinking separately as they emerge from each point.

The rustling of leaves in the wind becomes the whispering of voices, subtle and indistinct. More of them begin to speak all around me. Tens, hundreds, thousands of voices, all muttering to each other. Eyes poke out between the leaves, watching me hungrily. Amid the noise, I occasionally hear my name.

I turn back towards the stag. In an instant, the dissonant eyes on its antlers synchronize, all honing in on me. The energy I feel is a sudden and blinding hostility, a foul brew of hate and bloodlust and evil that scrapes at my skin, digs into me with venomous fangs. Their red pupils stare right through me, unblinking, reducing me to my most primal fears. I'm a caveman with a broken spear, staring down a predator that will eat me alive.

The whispers around me turn to murmurs, jeers, shouting, and screaming. I fall to my knees, clamping my hands over my ears as I try in vain to block out the deafening noise.

My dread transmutes into rage. I've been brought to my knees too many times in my life. I don't know where I am, but I know now that it's more than a dream. Something, somewhere, wants to torment me. But I've been tormented enough—abusive family, dismissive doctors, the trans-phobic bullies in high school and the adults who did nothing about it. I've survived this far in life just to spite them. I know I'm small, but I'm not fragile, and I never have been.

I glare up at the stag. I wish I could say something clever, but I've never been a poet. Instead, I growl through gritted teeth. "Fuck you."

The stag screeches, a demonic sound with a resonance that assaults me like a thousand needles from every direction. I roar in pain, but I refuse to budge. The beast explodes into a million shrieking shadows, whirring through the air in a volatile tornado. They freeze, then stretch into the silhouettes of razor sharp blades, all of their tips pointed at me. A moment of stillness passes, and I hear the faint wings fluttering near my ears. The blades launch themselves at me with bullet speed, and I brace myself for the assault.

Right before they tear me to shreds, a flock of birds sweeps in front of me, hundreds of small sparrows whirling around me in a shield of cinnamon wings. They drop out of the air one after the other as they take the blows from the blades, sacrificing themselves to protect me from the onslaught. As I succumb to the violent noise, my vision fading, a pit of rage opens up in my gut. The injustice of watching these fragile creatures slaughtered in droves by this formless evil, fills me with fury. I try to get to my feet, intent on finding the malevolent thing and making it bleed, but I lose consciousness before I get the chance.

CYCLE 3

I wake in my room, and immediately clap my hands over my ears again. I can barely hear the sparrows chirping through the shrieking. I scream in pain, but the hundreds of voices are so loud I can't even hear myself.

Desperate to end the noise, I look around my room, to find either its source or else a sharp item to stab my eardrums out with. I spot something that I've never seen before, and as I look towards it, the voices begin to fade. The relief is instantaneous, drugging me into bliss.

The thing that stands where my desk used to be is an altar made of muscle and bone. Pulsing blood vessels wind through the fleshy panels, disappearing under a frame made of ribs, femurs and humerus. Black candles are arranged on its surface in a seven-pointed star formation, with a scalpel lying in the center.

When I turn my head away from the altar, the screeching returns. I look back at the altar for relief, and as I stare at the red, pulsing fixture, an idea floats into my head. If I carve my heart out and place it on the altar, the voices will go away. So will my antisocial personality, my ADHD, my bipolar disorder—all of it. Every ailment I suffer from will be gone, forever. I don't know how, I just know it, as sure as snow is white.

Memories of my worst moments pass through my head. All of my hospital visits, doctors who dismissed my bipolar mood swings as "a result of my female hormones," case workers who gave up on me and shoved me off onto their coworkers because they thought I was too difficult. The long nights weathering manic episodes, seeing demons flying around my bed, watching my mirror reflection scream at me, hiding under my covers convinced my stuffed animals would come to life and strangle me. Everything the system has put me through, everything my own mind has devised to torment me. Now, I'm being presented with one cure for it all. How can I deny a chance like this?

Before I stand up, a hand grabs my shoulder. It's cold, leathery, with claws on the ends of its fingers. It whispers fiercely, "Don't."

I swallow. "Are you the thing that's trapped me here?" I demand, between gritted teeth. "Why are you keeping me from the cure?"

"This won't cure you," it replies.

My throat tightens. "If the candles burn out, I'll miss my chance."

"Think about where you got that idea," it says.

"Nowhere, obviously," I reply, through gritted teeth. "This is a dream, dreams are just *like* that."

Its breath is hot in my ear. "You're not dreaming."

"Then what am I doing here?" I snap. My eyes burn as I hold back tears.

"Go back to the beginning," it replies, its voice softening. "What is the first thing you remember?"

I wince as the experience comes to mind. Masha digging her blade into my stomach. The agonizing pain, the need to scream, the inability to push the sound out of my throat. I try to remember any other details. There was something before that, as I was waking up from the sleeping drugs. Voices. A conversation between Masha and another person. Or at least, I assumed it was a person. But I remember now that its voice didn't sound human.

I recall what happened in the upside-down woods, and I realize my brush with the void must be at the hands of whatever was speaking to her. When we were younger, she had a way of making me fear death in even the most mundane of moments. A memory comes to mind—when I was four years old, I found her dissecting a rat in the backyard, hidden just behind the shed. She was cataloging its organs, laying them out like a stamp collection and humming to the tune of an early-2000's pop song. When I threatened to tell our parents, she said "you know, if they want to do something to humans, they test it on rats first." It wasn't always something serious that would cause her to threaten me, either—one time I told her to stop chewing her food so loudly, and she replied with "I know the combination to dad's gun lock." In hindsight, she was probably lying half the time she made these comments, but the truth of it wasn't the point. What mattered was the quiet part, the words that remained unspoken. *I could kill you at any time, I just choose not to.*

Masha had somehow tapped into a dark power, the kind she would do anything to have. It would allow her to make good on every threat, to follow her every gruesome whim with little to no consequences. A creature of macabre impulse, stripped of all limitations. And if Masha really did summon some arcane evil out of hell to torment me, then it implied something I hadn't considered until now. That incident, her carving my insides out, hadn't been a nightmare at all. Unlike the last two dreams, that one must have been real, which means that somewhere, right now, I'm bleeding my guts out.

Voice shaking, I finally speak. "I'm dying, aren't I?"

"Not if I can help it," the voice says. "If you die, the ritual will be complete. Whatever you do, don't die."

"What am I supposed to do?" I ask. "I can't stop the bleeding from inside a dream."

"You have more time than you think," it replies. "So long as you don't give up."

"Give up on what?"

"On living," it says. "The moment you *choose* to die, there is nothing anyone can do to save you."

Its meaning is clear. There's a chance I can survive, but only if I keep choosing to take it. And that means fighting for my life—literally. I swallow anxiously. "Who are you?"

It says nothing, but I hear a faint sound from behind me. The chirping of the sparrow. I remember the flock of birds swirling around me, protecting me from the dark blades in the forest. I consider saying its identity aloud, but if it's protecting me, then I don't want to draw my adversary's attention to it. "What is this evil thing?" I ask.

The Sparrow's breath catches, but it doesn't speak. I'm about to ask my question again when I feel its talons grip my shoulder tighter. I look at the candles, and realize they've melted down, dripping off the edges of the altar.

Lines of wax begin to run down the sides, getting thicker as they wind along the floor, towards me.

My eyes go wide, and I try to get up, only to be assaulted by deafening shrieks once I turn away from the altar. I collapse again, unable to look away as the rivers of wax creep ever closer. They begin to crawl up my feet, burning the skin on my soles and ankles. I yelp in pain, trying to kick and scrape the wax off, but it continues to swallow me. I'm forced to look down, away from the altar, and the shrieking begins again, now joined by my own screams and curses as the wax crawls up my thighs.

The hot liquid stings and burns as it smothers me in blackness, now rushing in liters up my body, encasing me and my scorched flesh in a layer of wax. It pries my mouth open and crawls inside, and I try frantically to spit it out. But it keeps going, melting my tongue as it claws down my throat. My screams turn to agonized gargles as the wax chokes me.

Behind me, I hear a massive whooshing noise, followed by a rush of air that blows my hair and clothes forward. In an instant, the candle flames flicker out. The wax begins to cool and harden. As I lose consciousness, I look back up at the altar. The shrieking doesn't stop this time, and I realize the Sparrow was right—the promise of a cure was just a delusion, a lie conjured by the dark warden of this endless gauntlet of nightmares.

CYCLE 4

When I wake up again, it feels the way waking up normally does. For the first time, I don't hear chirping outside my window. I wonder if it all really was a dream. I think back on everything that happened, and when I find I can remember it all as clearly as real life, my excitement vanishes. I check my phone—again, the text is a jumbled mess. I'm still trapped.

Having realized this, I worry about the lack of chirping outside my window. If the Sparrow—or whatever it is—really does want to help me, then its absence is a problem. Best case scenario, it's keeping a low profile for now, in order to avoid this awful creature finding it. Worst case scenario, the creature already found it. I remember the sight of hundreds of birds dropping dead out of the air, impaled by a barrage of blades, and rage claws at my ribs. Who the Sparrow is, what they want, all of that is a mystery to me. But that kind of senseless killing, committing a heinous act against innocent creatures, is something I can't let go.

I know I want to fight this thing, but first I have to survive it, with or without the Sparrow's help. Excluding the last dream, every time I nearly died occurred after I left my room. I figure if I stay here and don't do anything risky, the creature will have less opportunities to torment me. It's not a perfect plan, but it's the best I have at the moment. I'll just pretend it's a normal lazy day.

I open the drawer beneath my bed and pull out my laptop. Strangely, I can see every sticker on it, and none of them are jumbled. I examine them closer, but I quickly realize they aren't what I remember. What should have been the My Chemical Romance logo now reads "My Time Has Come," and my Sonic the Hedgehog sticker has far too many eyes. The pokeball decal my friend gave me a few months ago is now slightly opened, with realistic guts falling out. When I squint, it almost looks like they're pulsing.

I give it the middle finger, then open my laptop. The text is still jumbled, and the desktop background has changed to an image of a bloated corpse, but I can still make out the Chrome icon on the taskbar. I navigate to YouTube—I figure I can waste my time watching videos, whether or not the creature continues to mess with them. I'm not the most extreme antisocial personality, but I'm low enough on empathy that graphic images of people being harmed don't usually bother me. And, if anything this evil creature throws on my screen does bother me, I can just click on another video. A boring strategy, but it will keep things manageable for me while also forcing the evil thing to stretch its imagination. I reckon it's similar to a cell in a video game, where the more items it has to load, the longer it will take, until it eventually bugs out and crashes. And if I can get it to crash enough, it might stop functioning altogether, breaking the cycle of nightmares. If nothing else, it'll stall for time until someone in my waking life can rescue me for good.

I browse through this crude imitation of my YouTube homepage, scrolling across thumbnails of gruesome scenes mixed with half-snatched images of videos I've seen before. As time goes on, the evil thing's strategy seems to change, and instead it begins filling the videos with personal threats. I don't know if it realizes how funny it is to show a YouTube thumbnail of someone trapped in a cage, with a red circle and arrow pointing to it followed by text that reads "THIS IS YOU," but it takes everything in me not to start laughing.

I open a few videos that I've watched several times, unsurprised to find that they start changing halfway through into something out of my weirdest fever dreams. Bass-boosted videos of someone noisily chewing their cereal, Joe Biden getting kinky with his anime clown girlfriend, 5-minute Crafts videos about how to make reusable diapers out of cow skin (complete with shrill upbeat corporate music). Finally, after opening a video of John Sakars repeatedly throwing himself into a wood chipper, I can't hold it in anymore. I burst out laughing.

The screen freezes, save for the buffering wheel. A new video starts. The thumbnail is for an episode of Last Week Tonight, a show I haven't watched in two or three years. It features the host, John Oliver, sitting behind a desk next to a graphic with the words "Ritual Sacrifice," pasted over an image of a pentagram with candles around it. I let it play.

"Our main story tonight concerns ritual sacrifice," John Oliver begins. "Humans have done it since the dawn of time, in just about every part of the world from the Romans to the Aztecs, and to this day it's a trope we see in horror movies. So tonight, we will talk about ritual sacrifice, its relevance in the modern day, and what you and I can do to help."

He says his final line with a gesture pointing towards the camera in a way that reminds me of those old Uncle Sam posters—ironic, coming from a smarmy British guy.

"When most people think of ritual sacrifice, they think of something like this," he says, gesturing to the camera. The screen cuts to a scene from a horror movie featuring a blonde woman in a white dress, shackled to a stone table in a dungeon and surrounded by torches. Seven hooded figures surround her, carrying upside down crosses and chanting in Latin. One of them takes a ceremonial dagger out of an ornate chest, then carves out the woman's heart, shown in slow, painstaking detail.

"And indeed, that's how most sacrifices go," says John Oliver as the screen cuts back to him. "That is, unless you're Ronald McDonald; then you just feed the sacrifice hamburgers until she dies from a stomach rupture." A photoshopped graphic of Ronald McDonald shoving a hamburger down a woman's throat appears on screen, and John Oliver does his most cringeworthy signature bit: turning to the graphic and shouting at it. "Ronald, stop it! She's had enough, Ronald!"

He returns to the subject at hand. "To properly begin a sacrifice, you must first inflict wounds that cause pain while preventing death, to maximize the victim's suffering—such as cuts, lashes, or breaking small bones in the extremities. From there, you cut the victim open, according to which organ you want to take."

Diagrams appear on screen, the first demonstrating a cut across the abdomen, just beneath the ribs. "This is the cut you would use to take out the liver, which is just under the diaphragm. It can be hard to get to since it's buried under other organs, so experience is required for this." Another diagram crops up on screen, showing Y-shaped cutting lines spanning from the chest to the pelvis. "This one, often called an autopsy cut, allows the sacrificer more choices of what they can cut out, but may cause the victim to die quicker."

His eyes begin running with blood, and his voice lowers into a growl. "The feeling of their bones being directly exposed to the air will already be agonizing, and as the sacrificer, you can compound this pain further by cutting into the sternum, ideally with a saw."

John Oliver grins maliciously. "From here, a sacrificer can do anything," he says. "They might pull your intestines out and arrange them on the floor in occult symbols, they might snip your blood vessels and use them to paint pictures, they might peel your skin off and blindfold you with it, feast on your liver, eat your eyeballs like cocktail cherries, ferment your blood into an unholy wine and force you to drink it, smear your shit on the walls"—foam appears at the corners of his mouth, his forked tongue flickering with delight behind his sharklike teeth—"all for the hedonistic delirium of mutilating your pathetic corpse for the pleasure and power of an all-consuming void that will slowly devour and digest you until you're nothing more than a primordial soup at the bottom of a lake of fire—"

He stops at last, then takes off his glasses, leaning closer to the screen and staring right at me. He shakes his finger in my direction. "And that is why you're here, Thaddeus."

I glare at him. "You're the one responsible for this, aren't you?"

John Oliver chuckles and leans back in his swivel chair. "No, that would be Masha," he says. "I'm just toying with you while I wait."

"You're doing a great job," I reply with a sneer. "I'm having a blast. That was funnier than any episode of Last Week Tonight I've ever seen."

"I suppose I should have expected your sense of humor to be just like your sister's," John Oliver replies. He shrugs. "But it doesn't matter. I know what she fears, and I reckon you fear the same things."

"What do you want, John Oliver?"

"That's not my name."

"Then what is your name?"

"I don't feel like telling you yet."

"Then I'll call you John Oliver until you do."

John Oliver sets his glasses aside and interlaces his fingers. "You're quite headstrong, aren't you?"

"I don't have patience for pathetic edgelords who think they can threaten me from behind a screen," I say. "Come out and fight me like a man, or whatever you are."

"You think you can kill a god, do you?" John Oliver says, with a smirk. "Prove it, then. Allow yourself to die, and you can come to my realm and fight me personally. You're apparently foolish enough."

A wry smile takes shape on my face. "You can't come out into our world, can you?" I say. "Not without a sacrifice. And my stupid sister didn't even finish the job." I chuckle. "Man, how embarrassing for both of you."

"I would say the same about you," John Oliver retorts, with a scowl, "given you've only survived this long with someone else's help."

I hear chirping outside my window again, but I'm careful not to react. I may not trust the Sparrow—I don't even know what it really is—but at the moment it's my only ally. I figure if I keep John Oliver's attention on myself, the Sparrow can help from the sidelines.

"How do you know I can't kick your ass if you don't come out of the screen and face me?" I taunt. "Come on, do it."

"Oh, I'm going to enjoy tormenting you for eternity," John Oliver replies, baring his teeth.

I toss the laptop on my bed and get up, raising my voice. "Come and get it!" I raise two middle fingers at him. "Fuckin' coward!"

"Careful what you wish for, Thaddeus," John Oliver replies, clicking his tongue. "The deeper I crawl into your mind, the more I can make you suffer—and the more powerful I grow. Are you sure you can beat me then?"

"Only one way to find out."

John Oliver bares his teeth in a too-wide grin, resting somewhere in the uncanny valley. "I look forward to it."

The laptop screen goes black. I tap on the trackpad, mash the power button, plug and unplug the charger. Nothing. That doesn't matter to me, though—there are other ways I can stretch his imagination, and I don't need to leave my room to do it.

I unlock my phone and navigate to Spotify, then pull up the album Savage Sinusoid by Igorrr—the most bizarre and complicated breakcore music I can think of. I tap on the first track, Viande, only for it to immediately turn into Shake It Off by Taylor Swift. I frown. Not the song I hate most, but definitely one of the more annoying pop songs in existence. I try tapping on a different track on the Igorrr album, Robert, only for it to immediately switch to Shake It Off again. Song after song, album after album. They all change into Shake It Off.

Frustrated, I open the YouTube app on my phone. I tap on a video I've seen a million times, only to find myself watching one of those annoying PETA ads showing pictures and videos of abused animals. Not the funny gore I watched earlier. My eye twitches. Every time I have to see one of their ads, showing abused animals in a fetishistic way, my gut twists with revulsion. This time is no different. I open other videos, but PETA keeps invading everything I tap on. Disgusted, I throw my phone aside. Whatever. I'll find something else to do.

I pull my sketchbook and pencil out of the drawer beneath my bed, and open to a fresh page. I barely manage to draw one line before the tip of my pencil breaks. I sharpen my pencil—which, of course, takes far longer than it should—then go back to the paper. My pencil barely touches the page, and the tip breaks again. I repeat this three more times, until finally throwing my pencil at the wall.

I pull out my guitar, but no amount of tuning can get it to sound right. When I paint my nails, I keep messing up and getting nail polish on the sides of my fingers. I try texting Matthias about my current dilemma, but when I try to type the word nightmar— nightmae— nightmre— *nihtmare— IGHTMRE—* I roar and throw my phone at the wall. I realize what's being simulated now is a stress dream. Worse than a nightmare, in my opinion.

I exhale harshly. So John Oliver wants to be petty, does he? Fine. Maybe I can't make things, but I can certainly destroy them.

I storm over to my closet and throw the doors open, revealing my drawers of art supplies—paints, markers, colored pencils. Hundreds of them. If this room is just one of John Oliver's creations, then it'll be hard for him to conjure hundreds of pencils falling in a chaotic pattern, the same way it would be difficult for a computer to render that many models. Besides, this isn't my real room. Who cares if I wreck it?

With a self-indulgent grin, I rip the top drawer out of its place and fling its contents across my room, sending hundreds of colored pencils flying through the air. But as I watch them, the morbid glee of destruction starts to fade. When they all land on the ground, I kneel down for a closer look. All of the pencils are gray. I blink, then look up at the rest of my room—posters, curtains, clothes, everything is gray. All of the color has been sucked out of it.

The lack of color is annoying at first, but if Evil John Oliver is taking elements away, that means my plan must be working. The more I give him to chew on, the more worn out he'll get, and I have other ideas. I go to my desk drawer and retrieve my utility knife, then approach my mirror. I almost don't recognize myself in grayscale, but the reflection still has all the detail I expect. One of the hardest visual graphics to simulate is a mirror reflection, because it essentially means creating not one, but two renders of the same scene. If it shatters, then that's even more renders, compounded by the number of pieces it breaks into. Including this detail must be particularly difficult for John Oliver. Perfect, for my purposes. I raise the butt of the knife, then bash it against the mirror.

I feel the impact rippling up my arm. I see the cracks appear in the glass and warp my reflection. But I don't hear anything. I slam my knife into the glass again, again, again, harder each time. It finally shatters, pieces flying out in every direction and coating the floor in tiny reflective shards. I still hear nothing.

I throw my nail polish at the wall, stomp on my bottles of paint, rip up my sheets and curtains—destroying anything and everything I can in this half-remembered facsimile of my room. The more I destroy, the more my vision blurs, until it vanishes altogether. In my frenzied rampage,

I stub my toe and trip on my desk chair, collapsing onto the floor. Even that sensation disappears, and I realize I can't even feel the ground beneath me, or the clothes on my skin. I'm in a void, deprived of every sense.

Hours pass. At least, it feels like hours. It could be days, weeks, years. Without my senses, I'm confronted with the blankness of eternity, and the existential horror that follows. I thought I knew what it meant to feel alone, but I didn't. I could never have known until now. Even when I felt alone in the past, there was always something else there. The noise of cars going by outside, the glitter of streetlights reflecting off the snow, the hearty taste of a frozen pizza after a long night, the smell of incense. The signs of life were there to comfort me even when I didn't realize it. Now, even those things are gone.

I blink, and sensation floods back to me. Colors, smells, sounds, pain, everything all at once. My heart rams against my ribs and my lungs try fruitlessly to keep up. Bits of shattered mirror bite into my back, and my whole body clenches in pain. As I'm wracked by violent convulsions, a dark figure rises up in front of me, tall and looming, with five-pointed antlers. Its twelve eyes stare down at me, crackling red and orange like dying stars.

"You think you can survive this?" the figure demands, an unholy timbre to its voice.

"I know I can," I snap back.

I try to get up and fight through the pain, but a sudden force whips me off the ground and drags me into the ether.

CYCLE 5

When I open my eyes, I'm floating above myself. I stare down at my mutilated body, guts splayed out around the operating table as the surgeons attempt to stitch my organs back together. The doctors had cut open my sweater and t-shirt, and my blood-soaked pajamas were torn off and tossed to the side. In the corner is a growing pile of bloody towels, which they're using to mop up every kind of discharge that issues from me. I'm hooked up to various tubes: anesthetics, blood transfusion packs, oxygen tanks and monitors. The chief surgeon barks orders at the rest of the staff as he works, using jargon I can't understand.

"Look upon your broken body, Thaddeus, and despair!" the Antler Man roars, his booming voice shaking the tableau before me. "You would put your fate in the hands of these fools?"

My spirit ripples when he speaks. I try to shout back, but I have no voice.

"Even if there were the slightest chance that these mere mortals could mend your wounds," the Antler Man continued, "do you think your life will ever be the same?" His voice grows louder, battering me from all sides. "You'll be a husk! A shell! Exiled from the pleasures of life and confined to an existence of misery!"

As he speaks, something within me vanishes. I look down at the body on the table, ginger curls spiraling out around its head, freckles and patchy stubble dotting its bloodless face. A large cut on the inside of its leg is already stitched up—likely an artery they had to close in order to prevent any more blood loss. The chief surgeon moves my organs aside, being careful not to nick any blood vessels. He examines the damage to the liver, which lies just beneath the body's diaphragm, near the top of its abdomen. The thing looks mangled. More than half of it has been hastily carved out, and what remains is marred with jagged cuts.

"Why open the whole abdomen if all they wanted was the liver?" one of the technicians remarks as she tosses aside a towel.

Another technician hands the chief surgeon the sutures he needs, and he begins working on a puncture in the stomach. "Same reason any psycho does this stuff," he says, with a grim expression. "They just want to see what's inside."

As I stare down, I come to understand that I am separate from the thing before me, the thing I recognize as myself. A chill grips my astral form. If that's Thaddeus, then who am I?

A visceral emptiness crawls through me. My life, my blood, my beating heart, are in the hands of doctors that I have learned not to trust. I realize I don't trust anyone, not even the Sparrow, to rescue me. I've buried myself under so many layers of armor that I can't remember who I was beneath it. Thaddeus is still alive according to the steady beeping of the monitors. But now, without my armor, I wonder if I'm already dead inside.

Before I can move closer, a sweeping sensation drags me into darkness. "I'll put you through as many nightmares as necessary, Thaddeus," says the Antler Man. "I will break you."

CYCLE 6

I'm staring out the front window of a bus, careening towards a sharp turn on the side of a mountain. The edge is so sheer that there isn't even a slope from the side of the highway, just a vertical drop. The valley is so far below that it's obscured by fog, and all I can make out is the silhouette of mountains in the distance dotted with pine trees.

I realize I'm in the driver's seat of the bus, and I stomp on the brake pedal. No response. I turn the steering wheel, pull the emergency brake—still nothing, still barreling towards the edge of a mountain. Behind me, children squeal, their voices like needles in my eardrums. I look back into the cabin of the bus, to find that it's all children.

I'm behind the wheel of a school bus. They scream louder, and I struggle to concentrate.

At the back of the bus is an emergency door, with a small oblong window showing the road behind us. Something flutters by it, and although I can't tell for sure if it's the Sparrow, I decide it's better than staying here. I step out from the driver's seat and make a break for the back door.

The children leap out of their seats, swarming me and grabbing at my clothes. They're still screaming, loud enough to be painful. I try to plug my ears again, but the children pry my hands away. "You're not real!" I shout as I elbow my way through them. It doesn't matter how loud I shout, my voice isn't audible over their shrieking. I've always hated children, and as they try to drag me back, it occurs to me that the Antler Man might know this. He hadn't demonstrated much personal knowledge of me up until now. I worry he may be delving deeper into my mind.

I fight my way to the back of the bus, shoving, kicking, punching my way through the mob of screeching children. "You're not real!" I shout. "None of this is real!"

At last I reach the emergency door, and grasp for the lever. The children are piling onto me now, their many hands gripping my arms and digging into my skin. They begin drawing blood—I realize their fingernails are morphing into claws, and their screaming is turning into inhuman howling. A rush of adrenaline pulses through me, and I struggle harder. I refuse to let the Antler Man win.

I roar, tug my arm free and grasp the lever. With a thunk, it unlatches and flies open. Outside, I see glimpses of fluttering in my peripheral vision. I grip the edges of the door and pull, trying to tear myself away from the horde of demons behind me. Blood drips on the floor as they scrape their claws across my skin, ripping it open in hundreds of jagged cuts.

A swarm of sparrows sweeps through the bus, pecking and clawing at the demons' eyes. I finally pull myself free, and dozens of tiny bird talons grasp my clothes right before I faceplant into the asphalt, rescuing me inches from impact.

"We'll keep doing this, Thaddeus." The Antler Man's voice pierces the void. "Over and over, until you finally understand how futile your struggle is."

CYCLE 7

Frigid wind and snow whip at my skin, piercing through every layer of my clothes. I know I'm going to die if I stay in this cold. And worse, I've been here before. This is a memory, a distinct one, full of desperation.

My hands are so numb it takes me a few seconds to realize I'm holding my old blue flip phone. It's open in my hand. Already dialing my dad. In my memory, I called him and asked if he could pick me up, since it was too cold to continue walking home. His reply still echoes in my head years later. "If you want to be a man, then start acting like one," he said. "Suck it up and find your way home." In hindsight, I didn't know what else I expected.

When this happened in my waking life, all I did was go to the closest gas station and call my Baba, who ordered a cab for me. It took an hour longer than it would have if my dad had done it, and a less jaded version of myself might have brought that up to him when I got home. But if I learned anything from this experience, it was that no amount of calling him on his bullshit would change anything. If he was so lazy that he would rather make up a transphobic excuse than hop in the car and drive twenty minutes to pick me up, then he was too lazy to be a better father.

I don't care to relive that experience, despite what the Antler Man may want. What he fails to realize is that putting me into these memories isn't purely distressing. It also gives me the opportunity to do what I wish I had done in the moment.

My dad's staticky voice comes through the phone. "What is it?"

"J-just wanted to t-tell you you're a p-p-piece of shit loser and I h-hope you f-fucking die in a h-high speed car c-crash," I bark, fighting my chattering teeth.

"The hell is that supposed to mean?" he barks back.

"You h-heard me, asshole!"

"The moment you get back here I'm kicking your ass!"

"You're n-not real, idiot!" My ears and fingers start draining of blood, snot freezing to my nose, mouth drying up from the cold air. "I'm not g-gonna fall for this s-s-stupid illusion, Antler Man!" My voice cracks into something between a growl and a wheeze. "You c-can't do shit unless I g-give up, and I'm n-never going to give up! I have e-every advantage, and y-you know it!"

The Antler Man speaks again, through the voice of my father. "The more you resist me, the more time I have to mine your worst memories and force you to relive them."

"Eat shit and d-die," I growl. I snap the phone shut, and a blast of snow and frigid air assaults me head on. My vision fades, and once again, I fall into the void.

"I have all the power here," the Antler Man says, his voice ripping through the darkness. "Your dreams are mine, and your body will be soon enough. You will lose your last shred of hope. All mortals do."

CYCLE 8

I'm standing at the edge of the hallway that leads to our back door. It's taller than I remember—or maybe I'm shorter. I look down to find I'm dressed in the pink overalls I wore religiously when I was little. I open the door to the backyard and look around the corner where Masha is doing something with her back turned. I remember where I am, and my blood runs black.

A whirlwind of malice consumes me. My heart bangs against my chest as I fight back tears, clenching and cracking my fists. In an instant, I see it with the same clarity as I did all those years ago. Our family cat's ears poking out from behind Masha. His lifeless head flopped to the side.

"Shadow!" I shout.

I was eight years old when this happened. I wanted to attack her, but I was too scared to do anything. I knew nothing about the world other than what kinds of consequences my parents might inflict. I was silent for weeks. Only my Baba realized something was wrong, and she wrestled the truth out of me. She let me stay with her for a while afterwards, justifying it by saying her arthritis was acting up and she needed help around the house.

Masha turns, and I see all of the unspeakable things she did to him. I feel so many emotions all at once—grief, betrayal, fear, despair, and a new thing I haven't felt before. Only now, almost thirteen years later, have I come to understand what it is. Empathy. Masha could torture me all she wanted. She could even cut me open. I didn't care. But seeing what she did to Shadow that day filled me with a whole new kind of fury, my vision turning red. To this day, I still want to kill her for what she did. And this time, I'm not afraid of the consequences.

"What's wrong?" Masha asks, devoid of remorse.

"How dare you, Masha?!" I shout, my voice cracking with anger. "How fucking dare you?!"

She giggles, enjoying my reaction. "Mom says we can't say that word—"

"You don't deserve to breathe air, you fucking monster!" I shout, my vocal cords giving out altogether and turning my voice into something between a wheeze and a roar. I pounce on her, my eyes burning with tears. "I'll kill you!"

She shoves back. "Get off me, Talia!"

I slap her, hit her, scratch at her face. "I'll kill you!" I repeat, screeching my words between blows. "I'll fucking kill you!"

As I tackle and pummel her, I hear birds flying around me. I don't care. She murdered Shadow. I want her to feel that pain a thousand times over. A faint voice tells me to stop. I don't stop. I need her to hurt for what she's done.

A sharp pain pierces my neck. I clutch the wound, and blood gushes out between my fingers. I realize Masha grabbed the scalpel during my frenzy and stabbed me with it.

She speaks, but the Antler Man's voice comes out. "I'm an unstoppable force," he says, grinning through Masha. "And you are not the immovable object you think you are. You're mortal, and one way or another, all mortals break."

I can feel the blood leaking down my throat now. It won't be long before it suffocates me. But I can't let him win. I grab the scalpel and rip it out of my neck. Before Masha can escape, I drive it straight into her jugular vein. I rip it out, and her blood sprays my face. I feel lightheaded.

I stab her again. It's not enough. I feel my skin getting colder. Again. Again.

I continue stabbing her, until I black out from blood loss.

CYCLE 9

I wake up in my bed, pulled into consciousness by the Sparrow's chirping. I no longer resent it—it's the one grounding thing I've experienced thus far, and at the moment, it's a relief. Stabbing the Antler Man in the neck with a scalpel seems to have hampered his power a bit, although I don't plan to get too comfortable. I now know that staying in my room won't keep me safe—he proved he can easily place me in any setting he wants, so there's no point in making myself stir crazy. I might as well pretend it's a normal day. I get up and put some clothes on, then head for my door.

When I step out of my bedroom, I hear retching coming from the bathroom just across the hall. Inside, I find my mother puking into the bathtub. She's sitting in a pool of her own urine, her scrubs stained with excrement as her body evacuates itself. "Thaddeus," she mutters between gags and retches. "Thaddeus, help—get my medication..."

Another memory. The last time this happened, I must have been around twelve years old. I remember searching for her nausea medication, and when she finally made it into her robe and back to her bed, I asked her what had happened.

"I just took too many meds, sweetie."

"But if you took too many, why did you need more?"

She didn't reply. At the time I assumed she dozed off, but looking back on it now, I think she only pretended to fall asleep because she couldn't come up with a convincing lie.

Now, I watch her heave her guts out with indifference. I'm pretty sure at this point she only keeps her job as a nurse because it allows her to steal morphine, and if that's the case, then these are the consequences of her actions. They are not, and never should have been, my problem. Maybe it's the APD, but I can't see her as anything other than pathetic, and I've lost all ability to forgive her.

"You're not real," I say flatly. "And you're not worth my time."

I shut the door on her and head downstairs to put on a pot of coffee, but when I step into the kitchen, the first thing I see on the counter is the knife block. My mind's eye conjures an image of all the blades flying out and impaling me, and I realize there are too many ways this could go wrong.

I wander around the rest of my house, looking for something to do that won't put me in too much danger. My living room looks the way it normally does—brown suede couch, plasma screen TV from 2013 hooked up to a Chrome stick, shelves of DVDs, framed family photos and knick-knacks. Before I sit on the couch, I feel a vague fear of something coming out from under the cushions and stabbing me, so I check beneath them. I'm relieved to find nothing but lint, change, and popcorn kernels from past movie nights.

Turning on the TV does nothing for me—all it plays is static, and the Chrome stick won't respond to the remote. I consider playing a movie on DVD, but the only available selection is my dad's collection of James Bond movies, and I'd rather watch paint dry. My phone barely functions, still covered in unreadable text and unable to play anything but

Taylor Swift and PETA ads. Exhausted of all options, I sit on the couch and stare into space.

To my right, a wooden crucifix hangs on the wall. It's a relatively crude wooden carving, but the craftsmanship wasn't what made my dad buy it—he bought it because it's an Orthodox cross. He thought we couldn't be a proper family without one, and the best he could get was this crudely carved wooden figure he found at a thrift store when I was a toddler. Not very easy to find Eastern Orthodox apotropaics, let alone anything Russian, in post-Cold War America.

I get tired of staring at the Jesus-adjacent art project hanging on the wall, and I start messing with things on the shelves. Vinyl records, snow globes, old toy dinosaurs. I pick up a glass figurine of an octopus, examining the blue and purple swirls of color along its surface. It's large and fragile enough that I have to hold it with two hands, and it's surprisingly heavy. It was a gift to my mother from a few of her friends—they told her it was Venetian glass, purchased on their trip to Italy that year. My mom never noticed the text on the bottom that reads "made in China."

I know better than to assume I'm safe in my house, and I'm tired of scanning my shelves for something to do. I decide to take a walk to the park instead. "Normal day," I mutter. "Just a normal day."

When I open the front door, I find a small camera crew standing in my yard, setting up around a blond man wearing a gray jacket and a red t-shirt. As I get closer, I realize he's a YouTuber I recognize—Tom Scott. I know he mostly does educational content, although I haven't seen many of his videos.

"What are you doing here?" I ask.

He doesn't answer. I ask again, and still I get no response. I tilt my head, then walk up to him and wave my hand in front of his face. He continues chatting with the cameraman, who's setting up a tripod on our lawn. I'm invisible to him.

Confused, I sit on a nearby bench and watch. They get into position, and with the clap of the film slate, the camera starts rolling and Tom Scott begins his lecture. "I'm just outside of the Morozov house," he says, reading off a teleprompter, "a historic home in Chicago that is said to be possessed by a dark god. The local legend goes that the eldest sister in the family, Masha, tried to summon the Russian pagan god of darkness, Chernobog. She did so through a ritual sacrifice, using her own sister, Talia."

I wince. It made sense when I got deadnamed in a memory from being eight years old, but hearing it out of Tom

Scott's mouth is irritating in a way I didn't expect. I reckon it's just another one of the Antler Man's attempts to get a rise out of me, albeit more subtle than the last dozen or so.

"The sacrifice was unsuccessful at first," Tom Scott continues, "thwarted in part by an early police response, and because of the intervention of Belobog, the light-god counterpart of Chernobog. The mythos surrounding these two is that they're constantly dueling each other, the light keeping the darkness at bay until the end of time. Had Belobog succeeded in keeping Talia alive, the legend may have been very different from what it is today."

"My name is Thaddeus, dipshit!" I shout.

Of course, he doesn't react. But I consider what he's saying. He's providing some answers that I've been wanting for a while now, along with a vision of the potential future, if I don't survive. It's annoying, but it's worth listening to.

"The past few years since it happened have not been easy for the rest of us," he continues. "From the necrotic plague spreading across the world to the increases in war and poverty, people everywhere have been trying to understand what caused so much darkness to fall over us in so little time. But—according to the residents of this suburb in Chicago, at least—the answer is quite clear."

I hear the Sparrow chirping, and it flies in front of him, interrupting the shot. He and his crew all make disappointed noises, then start over in a second take. I sit through it again, trying to pay better attention. The names Chernobog and Belobog ring a bell for me—I feel like I've heard Masha say them before. This must be why the Sparrow, or Belobog, wants me to live. For that matter, the slew of near death experiences the Antler Man, or Chernobog, just put me through, may have been a strategy to draw the Sparrow out of hiding. The closer he comes to killing me, the more Belobog has to come to my rescue, the more opportunities Chernobog gets to eliminate him somehow. Apparently, the one thing the Antler Man isn't able to count on is my own ability to fight back.

"In pre-Christian Slavic folklore," Tom Scott continues, "much of the way they perceived the world revolved around duality. Belobog and Chernobog represent more than just light and dark—they represent good and evil, peace and war, abundance and famine—" he ascends the steps to our porch, the cameraman following a few feet behind him "—creation and destruction."

I get up from my seat and follow them, curious where this is going. The way he speaks is more theatrical than how he started out, with bigger hand gestures and a wide, toothy smile. "Today, we're seeing the results of a world without Belobog." As he speaks, his skin begins chipping like paint, peeling itself off and falling away from him.

"One where creatures of the night reign over the living, where the *upyri* may feast on their blood with reckless abandon…"

I roll my eyes as Tom Scott talks. I've heard my Baba talk about *upyri* before—during her childhood in Russia, they were a real fear. "I didn't grow up in the motherland," I say, assuming the Antler Man can hear me. "I grew up here. They're called vampires, and in America, they sparkle."

Tom Scott doesn't respond, and I'm not going to push my luck in case he decides to later on—I don't really feel like sitting through a repeat of the John Oliver situation. I consider continuing my trip towards the park, but after hearing talk of a necrotic plague, I figure it's better to go back inside my house instead.

The moment I close the door behind me, I'm assaulted by voices in my head, shouting "die, die, I hate you, fuck you," over and over from all directions. I clap my hands over my ears, but they do nothing. The Antler Man is deep enough inside my mind now that he knows what my psychosis is like. And as I squint around the living room, I realize that means he knows what kinds of delusions I get as well.

The feeling overcomes me—a dead certainty that I'm not alone, and something in my house wants to kill me.

In my peripheral vision, I catch a glimpse of the Orthodox cross.

The crucified Jesus turns its head. Its crudely-painted wooden eyes stare at me like a wolf staring at prey, blood dripping from its crown of thorns. It rips its arm away from the cross, spraying blood on the end table beneath it as the stake passes straight through its hand.

To my right, I see motion on one of the shelves. The glass octopus stretches its tentacles out from around a corner. They grip the sides of the shelving unit, pulling its body forward until its buggy eyes emerge from around the corner. It turns and stares at me, blinking once, then undulates down the shelves and starts wriggling towards me.

I see more motion around the room. Hands reach out from picture frames, and the upper torsos of family members crawl out of them, digging their nails into the wooden floorboards as they drag their malformed bodies towards me. Mimics emerge from behind the furniture, mutated shadows of chairs and shelves and tables snarling and snapping their teeth as they lurch out of hiding and converge on me.

I bolt up the stairs to my room. The creatures ambulate after me, picking up speed. I slam my door behind me, just in time to amputate one of the octopus's tentacles. I lock my door and stomp on it over and over again, furiously smashing it under my heel until it's nothing more than a smear on the ground. I reach for my end table and gulp down my antipsychotic medication, taking one more than I should in my race to make the creatures go away.

The thumping against my bedroom door fades and stops as the medication dulls my neural synapses. I take a long, deep breath, then crawl under my covers. The sensation that follows is heavy, unpleasant. But at least it makes the chaos stop. My eyes drift closed, and before long, I'm out like a light.

CYCLE 10

As I float up into consciousness, I hear a mix of sounds. The Sparrow's familiar song, and a foreign, slimy sound, like someone trying to lick Nutella straight out of the jar. It grates on my ears, loud enough to keep me from sleeping. I finally crack my eyes open and roll over.

There's a horse in the middle of my room, grazing on a corpse's innards.

I frown. That's not right. When I look closer, I realize that the body on the floor is a doppelganger of myself. I figure this is probably one of the Antler Man's attempts to intimidate me. I decide to ignore it, rather than give him the reaction he wants.

No longer able to sleep, and becoming increasingly annoyed by the squelching and slurping sounds, I decide to leave my room. The horse is blocking the exit, because of course it is, and it won't budge regardless of how much I try to push it or spook it away. Eventually I find a way to climb around it and squeeze through the opening of the door.

I blink, and I'm in a hospital. The linoleum and plaster corridor diverges, one path leading to an exit and the other veering right. The doors are heavy slabs of steel, like gates to a tomb. I look down to find I'm wearing loose-fitting, flimsy scrubs and yellow ankle-cut socks, and I know where I am. No belts, no shoelaces, no plastic spoons to whittle into shanks. Crayola markers only in this wing of the hospital.

At the intersection of the hallways, two receptionists sit behind a corporate blue desk. Or, I think they're receptionists. It's difficult to tell, because their faces have been squashed flat like Play-Doh. They look up at me with their lopsided eyes, and their mouths move like they're trying to speak, although all that comes out of their mangled faces is a mess of unintelligible noises. One of them picks up a phone, watching me warily and muttering alien gibberish into the receiver.

Rushed footsteps echo down the hall. More of these creatures lumber around the corners and surround me, all wearing hospital scrubs and making loud whooping noises. They descend on me like yipping hyenas and restrain my arms. I kick and scratch and struggle, at one point sinking my teeth into one of them. I discover with revulsion that my teeth sink all the way in and pull out a chunk of their flesh, with the taste and texture of Play-Doh. I spit it out, coughing and gagging as they drag me into the psych ward.

A needle punctures my arm, flooding my veins with sedatives as they wrangle me, kicking and screaming, into the crisis room. The chemicals rush through me with every pump of my heart, dulling my nerves and muscles until my entire body goes limp. They set me down in one of the recliners along the edges of the room, tilting the seat up just enough so that I won't choke on my own saliva. I realize with distaste that they've incorrectly placed me on the women's side of the room, same as last time.

I strain to drag my thoughts out from the murk of the sedatives. I remember my last involuntary visit to the psych ward like it was yesterday—delusions that the other people around me were dead, hallucinating the meals they gave us being made of human toes, the unfunny reruns of Friends playing on all the TVs. The disquieting feeling of being trapped in a room with strangers who are just as unstable as you.

Finally, I can move my head slightly. I slowly crane it to the side so I can look at the woman next to me. It's the same woman as last time, minus the complaining about the Friends reruns—minus an entire face, in fact. She's dead, bloated and purple, with maggots wriggling around her tongue and excavating her eyes. I glance at the few other people in my field of view. Bodies everywhere, all littered around the room on flimsy recliners and thin foam mattresses, all rotting. Just food for the maggots.

Something grabs my face. One of the Play-Doh nurses cranks my head upwards and squeezes my jaw muscles, forcing my mouth open. My heart bangs against my rib cage as I try to fight the sedatives, to wrangle myself free. My limbs won't budge. The nurse drops something pill-shaped in my mouth, and I try to cough it out, but they flood my mouth with water before I have the chance. I lie there, helplessly, as the thing slides down my throat.

As I lie there in the recliner, dazed and drowsy from all the medication, my eyes start to close. And as I drift off to sleep, something begins to wriggle in my guts.

Cycle 11

I wake up in my room again, even groggier and achier than before. The horse is gone, thankfully, but the corpse of my doppelganger is still on the ground beside my bed. I see motion, and I squint, trying to get a better view. Pack rats, dozens of them, burrowing between folds of necrotic skin, pulling out fragments of bone and cartilage and spoiled meat to take back to their nests. I try to move, but my stomach is weak. I feel the same wriggling in my guts, and I recall those Play-Doh nurses forcing something down my throat. I swear I can feel it breeding within me. I realize I have to throw up, get it out of my system.

The moment I sit up, a wave of nausea rips through me. I clutch my stomach, choking back vomit. I jump out of bed, nearly tripping over the bag of skin and bones next to me as I race out my door.

What awaits me in the bathroom is a gut-twisting tableau that stops me in my tracks. What used to be my mother is now rotting in a pool of her own blood and excrement, surrounded by fat flies. The stench of her swollen corpse is so rank that I immediately contribute, voiding my guts all over the floor. Against my better judgment, I look at the contents of the vomit—black and tarlike, with maggots squirming around in it. Anxiety crawls up my throat as I realize what this means. They're eating away at my stomach lining, riddling me with ulcers. If it gets any worse, I'll start bleeding internally.

I know my mother has nausea medication somewhere in her bedroom, and I remember taking the same kind of medication the last time I had stomach ulcers. With no other ideas, I begin shuffling across the hall. My vision blurs as the nausea pulses through me, and my breathing becomes shallow as I try not to puke on my feet. I make it halfway through her room before ejecting what feels like a liter of black tar and worms onto my parents' blankets. At last, I reach her bedside table, fumbling around in the drawer until I find the medication. I pop two tablets under my tongue, then put the bottle in my pocket as I wait for them to dissolve.

I'm aware that I'm still in a manufactured nightmare, which means interacting with items in the setting is only going to do so much for me. But the medication seems to be helping somewhat, and that means it's not completely futile. It might be the subtle influence of the Sparrow trying to help me from a distance, or it might be my own memories conjuring these things. Either way, I'll take whatever help I can get.

My father hides his medications from my mother in his workshop, and I know he has something for heartburn. It won't do much about the maggots, but it'll reduce my stomach acid, and that ought to at least buy me a little more time. Once I start feeling a little better, I head downstairs, moving slowly so as not to upset my stomach again.

When I finally make it to the door, I realize I've made a mistake. The garage doesn't have heating. I consider going up to my room to get a heavier coat, but I can already feel the pain returning. I won't make it there and back before I'm no longer able to walk. I have to endure the Chicago winter.

I push open the door, and the cold stings my face. I know I can tolerate a few minutes of it, but it won't be long before I can't bear it anymore—I need to be smart about how I search. I try to walk quicker, but the motion twists my guts, forcing me to slow down again. I shuffle across the floor, moving as fast as I can manage while still keeping the tempest in my stomach at bay.

As I cross the garage floor, I look around at the shelves, trying to spot any containers he might hide the medications in. I figure he would want to store them somewhere close by his workbench, that way he can keep a better eye on them.

I finally make it to the other end of the garage, my hands gradually numbing as I open each of his drawers. It becomes harder to keep a grip on anything as my fingers stiffen and ache with the cold. The longer I search, the worse it gets.

I look up at the top shelves, but as I reach for a container, my stomach flips, and I have to stop and clutch my gut. The warmth my sweater provided me has vanished completely, the fabric cool against my arms. The cold sinks into my skin, biting my nerves. My body shakes like a skyscraper in a low grade earthquake. I shuffle over to my dad's rolling tool cabinet, fighting through my nausea. When I touch the metal drawers, the cold crawls up my fingers like a hundred spiders. I wince at the sensation. I try to rifle through them quickly.

My teeth chatter. My ears feel close to falling off. The cold air is like needles in my lungs. I keep my focus on the drawers—there's damn near twenty of them, each more disorganized than the last. My stomach roils again. I gag, pause, swallow. I reach for more nausea medication and pop another pill under my tongue. I continue searching.

I'm running out of places to look, and I can't tolerate this cold for much longer. Having exhausted all my other options, I root around in his toolbox. I find a false bottom, and after shifting as many of the heavy items as I can, finally pull it out. I laugh weakly. Of course it would be the last place I think to check.

I grab the antacids out of the pile of medicine bottles, then begin the long trek back to my room, clutching my stomach and willing my stiff joints to move. As I shuffle towards the door, feet stinging with every step across the frigid cement, I try to pull out a few of the antacids. My trembling hands struggle with the cap, and I curse when I drop a few. I realize I can't bend over to grab them, so I continue towards the door. I swallow a few of the pills dry, then put the bottle back in my pocket, not bothering to close it tight. If they spill, they'll just spill in my pocket. Right now, I don't have the luxury of caring about that.

When I make it inside, I slam the door behind me and wrap my arms around myself, trying to stop shivering. The furnace is a few feet away, and I stand in front of it for a while. Once again, the nausea returns, quicker than it did the last time. I know this medication isn't supposed to go through my system so quickly—I reckon the Antler Man must be counteracting the Sparrow's influence somehow. I decide to go back to bed and lie down.

Our house isn't the largest one in this suburb of Chicago, but the ten yards or so back to the stairwell turn into miles as I grow sicker. I feel like my stomach could disintegrate at any second. When I reach the stairs, a new, agonizing pain assaults me, and I grip the railing to stay upright. A thought enters my mind, cutting through the brain fog. *I need a doctor.*

The switch flips on in my head—a feeling I now recognize. The point you pass when a crisis turns into a near death experience. When you realize with piercing clarity that if you don't do something *right now*, you're going to die. The bleeding in my stomach isn't just another one of the Antler Man's tricks. Something awful is happening to my body right now, and only the doctors in the real world can fix it. Until they do, I'll be on the verge of death. And there's nothing I can do to control it. The pain worsens, and I groan involuntarily. My entire body trembles, and soon I'm too weak to stay standing.

Right before I fall, a pair of talons catches me under my arms.

"Don't give up," the Sparrow whispers fiercely. It steadies me, being careful not to touch my stomach. "If you give up at any point—if you doubt yourself for even a second—it's over." It grips me tighter. "You're so close, Thaddeus. Do *not* give up!"

"How do I..." I can barely talk, whispering my words between shallow breaths. "Know I can—can trust you..."

"Neither of us has a choice," it replies. "If you die, I die."

"I c—c..." the act of speech is agonizing, the mere vibrations in my chest radiating down to my eroding stomach. I can't do it anymore. Instead, I sign out my reply, using my limited knowledge of the ASL alphabet. N-O W-A-L-K B-C P-A-I-N.

The Sparrow understands. "My power is limited, but I can help."

I feel a light breeze around me, and the pain subsides just enough to allow me to continue. "Keep going," it says. A few birds fly out around me, gliding up the stairwell and passing through my bedroom door. "Follow the sparrows."

I take my first step. My stomach roars. I pause and take a deep breath. A memory from a few years ago surfaces in my mind, of getting lost while hiking alone and running out of water. I survived by focusing on finding water first, and getting back afterwards. One thing at a time. Faced with the problem of scaling this stairwell, I feel like I'm back there, climbing rocks to reach a spring. I look down at the step in front of me. *One foot in front of the other.*

I climb one step. Another. Another. I pause, beginning to feel off-center. Gravity is tilting. I look up again and realize that the whole stairwell is wobbling. I feel like I'm crossing a weathered rope bridge, waiting for it to tilt too far and send me plummeting into the vast canyon below. I repeat my mantra, returning my focus to the next step. *One foot in front of the other.* Another step. Another. The unsteady ground worsens my nausea, and I void my guts again, sending the black detritus over the side of the railing, where it lands on the floor in the living room. I wipe my lips, right myself, and continue.

From muscle memory, I know that I should be halfway there. But when I look up again, the stairs stretch out like an optical illusion. I see motion in my peripheral vision, and a swarm of scorpions crawls up the stairwell, thousands of them, spiraling out along the walls and ceiling. The Sparrow grips me tighter, shielding me from their stingers. "Keep going," it whispers.

I take another step. "What's at the to—" I gag, then swallow "—top of these stairs?"

"I don't know," it replies. "But the moment you give up, your heart stops beating." Another wave of healing energy surrounds me. "No matter what happens, you must keep moving!"

I groan, take another step. "The Antler Man must have—have something waiting for me..."

"Most likely," the Sparrow replies. "We are in his domain now. He writes the rules. Neither of us can predict what happens next. All you can do is survive."

Another step. I feel dizzy. I see a flash of the operation table, surgeons scurrying around my body and shouting at each other while the vitals machine goes haywire. The chief surgeon orders more blood transfusion packs, while a technician frantically replaces blood soaked towels. One of them grabs a defibrillator, powering up the machine and sticking the pads to my chest. "Clear!"

The jolt brings me back to the stairwell with a new rush of adrenaline. I climb three steps, but the nausea returns, and I have to slow down. I know I'm near the top. Only two more steps. A new shock of pain rips through me, and I clutch my stomach. I pause, wavering. If I do make it out of this alive, what will I wake up to? A terrible family, a broken body, no future. What do I have to live for, really?

"Keep moving!" the Sparrow hisses.

But why? My first thought is my Baba. But what happens when she dies? After being stabbed and gutted, will I be well enough to care for her when she's too old to do so herself? Well enough to do anything?

"Don't let him win!"

Another jolt hits me, bringing with it a renewed clarity. Even if I don't have any extrinsic reason to live, I do have something—spite. I imagine waking up, taunting Masha from outside of her jail cell. "They caught you. Fuckin' loser." I picture Masha lurking behind the bars. Her sullen face as I look her in the eyes and hiss, "Try harder next time." The idea fills me with venomous delight. Any reason to live is a good reason, even if it's just refusing to let the people who hurt you win—the drive to live on in spite of the forces that wish you were dead, to show them you cannot be conquered. I growl through the pain, and with every last shred of strength I have in me, push myself up the final step.

Something lifts inside of me. The nausea fades, and after taking a deep breath, I'm strong enough to stand on my own again. At last, I look up, reaching for my bedroom door. I don't know what awaits me, but I do know I can fight it. I twist the knob, and pull it open.

CYCLE 12

My room looks the same as I left it, with one key difference—the doppelganger corpse has been completely cleaned out. The horse ate its insides and the pack rats took everything else. Nothing remains except skin and clothes.

A nxiety twists my insides. I don't know what's wrong with this skin suit sprawled out on my floor, but my gut tells me I shouldn't go near it. I stand in my doorway, still, silent, watching the thing without blinking.

There's motion beneath it. Is it a leftover pack rat? I watch as the ripples and folds in the hide begin to unfurl, extending like rubber along the ground. What remains of its face becomes fully visible—a pale, leathery death mask surrounded by a mop of fraying ginger hair. The head tilts up at an unnatural angle, staring at me through the voids where its eyes used to be. No, it's not pack rats. The thing is alive.

Its flattened fingers grip the floor as it drags itself forward. Its mouth opens hungrily, and it begins maneuvering the flaps in its hide like a squid out of water. I back away slowly, not wanting to make any sudden moves.

The thing shoots out an arm, like a lizard striking a fly with its tongue. Before it can make contact with my ankle, a bird flies in front of it, blocking the strike. Hundreds of sparrows swoop in, swarming the skin suit and pecking it apart.

I whip around and slam the door behind me, only to find myself staring down an endless hallway. Fluorescent lights line the ceiling, illuminating the off-white plaster walls and checkered linoleum flooring with an eerie glow. A rush of shadows floods in, spiraling out and collecting in a pool a few yards in front of me. A figure rises out of the blackness, towering over me. His twelve crackling red eyes stare down at me, and the void of his face splits into a massive grin, baring thousands of razor-sharp teeth. A forked tongue slithers out and licks his lips as he raises his scythe.

Suddenly, a flash shoots out from behind me, piercing the black void with a spear of light. The Antler Man dissipates with a malicious hiss, before converging once more in pools of shadow. The Sparrow shouts a fierce command.

"*Run!*"

I bolt down the hall. The Antler Man's long strides and thundering footsteps shake the ground, growing louder as he chases after me. The hallway stretches and distorts, checkered tiles expanding and contracting. More birds shoot past me, and the Antler Man's heavy, lurching strides slow. Gut-rending grunts and growls echo down the hall as he fights the swarm of sparrows whirring around him. I feel a brief urge to look behind me, but I know the moment I do, I'm dead.

The floor continues to warp, optical illusions and shifting patterns making hills and pitfalls appear in the linoleum. As the Antler Man's strides grow louder again, a rush of air picks up beneath me. At once, I'm lifted off the ground, flying on wings that conjure themselves on my back. I glide on the gusts of wind until I see a doorway in the distance—an end to the hall. As I barrel towards my destination, the Antler Man roars after me, picking up speed. The fluorescent lights flicker, and the walls bend and twist around me. Before long, I'm hurtling through darkness.

Streams of light shoot ahead of me, illuminating my path in flames. A swarm of birds rushes me from my right, knocking me off my trajectory. A split second later, they're cleaved by the massive swing of a black scythe, a deadly strike which they narrowly saved me from. The blade buries itself in the linoleum. Still, I flee, surging ahead on ethereal wings.

With an ear-splitting roar, the Antler Man pulls his scythe out of the ground, then lumbers after me. The Sparrow's power is spread thin, and when the Antler Man gets close, I will have to fight on my own. When I feel his weapon graze me, I turn to face him.

The Antler Man swings, his massive weapon bringing a gust of air with it as it sweeps across the hall. I launch myself backwards with my wings, narrowly avoiding the strike. I dodge again, then again. I'm running out of breath. Each swing of the Antler Man's scythe is a potential killing blow. I don't know how far the door is behind me. My heart bangs against my ribcage. I'm starting to think I won't make it.

The Sparrow materializes once more, shoving me to the side again. I finally get a glimpse of my protector. Its four wings, coated in iridescent copper feathers, extend to shield me from our adversary. It has no face, only swirling wisps of light beneath a bejeweled bronze halo. I'm almost distracted by its beauty. But the moment doesn't last.

Another deadly blow—one that almost hits me—cleaves through the Sparrow instead. A horrible screeching noise splits the air as its glowing form explodes into shards of light. The Antler Man laughs, a rumbling noise that shakes me to my core. My protector is gone.

The flames begin to dim. I drop out of the air, my wings fading into nothingness. My adversary grows taller. Shadows stretch out along the hall as his glowing red eyes hone in on me. I can almost feel his fingers wrapping around my heart.

I scramble to my feet and race for the door. As I run for my life, the details of my surroundings blur, collapsing into a collection of gray lines and surfaces that become more indistinct with each step. The Antler Man's strides are fading behind me—am I outrunning him? Is he getting smaller? But I can't turn and look. I have to reach the end.

As I sprint ahead, I notice even the door is dissolving into gray lines and shapes, infected by the same vagueness as the hallway. I push myself harder, running faster than I ever thought I could. I reach out as I draw closer, watching the lines on the door fade into nothingness.

Right before it disappears, I grasp the handle.

CYCLE 00

My eyes flutter open. They're puffy and swollen, like I've been sleeping for days. The ceiling I'm staring at isn't my own—it's gray, illuminated by soft light from a window at the other end of the room. On my left is a curtain, the same sanitarium blue color that everything in a hospital seems to be—the blanket, the scratchy sheets of the bed I'm lying in, the few visitor chairs in the corner. My arm is hooked up to an IV, bruised and crusted with dried blood where the needle enters my skin. Something brushes my nose as I move, and I reach up to touch it—an oxygen feed. I yawn, but I can't stretch without it hurting.

S omeone gasps from the right side of the room. Beneath the curtains, I see a pair of suede black boots with thick heels rush in my direction. My mother throws aside the curtains, covering her mouth when she sees me. Tears form at the corners of her eyes, and she wipes them away with the sleeve of her gray cardigan. "Oh my God, you're awake!" She looks like she's about to hug me, but another voice interrupts her.

"Jennifer!"

My Baba walks up behind her. She looks, as always, exactly how a babushka should look—gray hair hidden under a floral-print veil, a wine red wool sweater and a long knit skirt. Her presence is the perfect combination of comforting and commanding, the way a grandmother who survived the war ought to be. She puts her hand on my mother's shoulder. "They just patched him up," she says, in her cigarette voice. "I can't have you squeezing the life out of him again."

"How did I get here?" I mutter, exhaling the cobwebs in my lungs.

"You don't have to worry about that," Mom says. "Just focus on healing."

I try to shift positions, but another volley of pain rips through me. I wince, clutching my abdomen. "It feels like someone carved me open."

"You're fine, Thaddeus," she says, with a conspicuously reassuring tone. "The doctors patched you up, and you're on your way to recovery."

I give her a sideways glance. I can tell she's deflecting. She doesn't want to talk about it. But it won't matter soon. Bits and pieces of what happened are already beginning to surface in my mind, memories of candles and incense and lines of salt. Masha, smiling serenely as she brandishes a knife.

"Why don't you go call Dmitri, hm?" Baba says. "Give him the news."

She nods. "Yes, of course, good idea." After a few seconds of fumbling with her purse, Mom pulls out her phone and steps outside to dial my father.

Baba pulls up the doctor's stool and sits in it, resting her hands on her brass cane and smiling at me. "I'm glad you're alive."

"It was Masha, right?" I croak.

She nods. "Some kind of absurd witchcraft, I hear." She gestures to me. "Thankfully, it didn't work."

"Because she's too stupid to pull it off," I grumble spitefully.

"Because you're strong."

A moment of silence passes as I take in her words, dragging what few thoughts I have out from the murk of fatigue. The more cynical part of me thinks this is just her nice way of saying I'm stubborn—but maybe stubbornness and strength are two sides of the same coin. I smile back at her.

"I waited here the whole time," Baba says. "Every day, the moment visiting hours started to the moment doors closed."

I glance at the small window on the door, where I can see my mother talking on the phone. "They have me on morphine, don't they?"

Baba follows my eyes, then looks back at me. She nods silently, and we share a look of understanding. Whether Mom is far gone enough to steal pain medicine from her own child isn't clear, but it's also not a possibility either of us will risk. Baba has always been wicked smart, and more than that, she's the only person in this shitshow of a family that I can actually trust. She protected me here. I make a silent promise to protect her, too, if the situation arises.

More memories return to me, and I look over at the table next to my bunk. "Hey, Baba," I say. "Did they happen to put my phone anywhere nearby? I need to check something."

"Yes, I thought you might want to tell your friends you survived," she says. She pulls my phone out of her purse and hands it to me.

My screen is flooded with notifications, mostly from friends on Discord. I see one from my friend Matthias. I swallow, then tap on it.

mayhematthias 01/07/2022 11:42 AM

```
hey i havent heard from you in a
while
```

```
thaddeus
```

```
answer me bitch
```

mayhematthias 01/07/2022 4:57 PM

```
i just checked your moms facebook
holy shit dude
```

```
its on the news too
```

```
a bunch of alt right chuds in the
comments on the article are talking
shit so ive been replying and calling
them fags
```

```
i figure thats what you would want
me to do anyhow
```

mayhematthias 01/08/2022 2:18 AM

```
i know youre insurgery right now and
thats why youre not replying
```

```
just please
```

```
say something when you wake up
```

The relief is like a sedative. I can read the text. That's one worry off my mind. I have one last test to do, and I start typing.

hellsfavoritenuisance 01/12/2022 10:33 AM
`i lived bitch`

I let out a breath I didn't realize I was holding. I can type, too. I think of one last response, and I type it up with a wry smile.

hellsfavoritenuisance 01/12/2022 10:34 AM
`and im gonna make it everyone elses problem`

I set my phone down and look up at Baba. "What happened to Masha?" I ask her.

"All I know is that she's in jail," Baba says with a sigh. "Your mother knows more about the charges and such, but she refuses to talk about it."

"She's in total denial about it. About most things in her life," I grumble. "What did the doctors say about me?"

"They said your liver is likely to grow back, and they gave us a printout of dietary restrictions to follow while it heals, although they didn't want to make any guarantees," Baba replies. "But, full recovery or not, I'll be here for whatever may come." She smirks. "In the meantime, I hope Masha has a very, very incompetent lawyer."

I start to chuckle, but the shooting pain stops me. I grimace, clutching my stomach. "God, I can't laugh," I groan. "Did the doctors even do their job right?"

"We can only hope."

She smiles radiantly, banishing the shadows out of the room for just a moment. A glimmer on her sweater catches my eye, and I realize she's wearing a brooch—a golden sparrow holding a sprig of wheat. I see a glimpse of those final moments running from the Antler Man. The screech of a bird, the slash of a scythe. A bright light, extinguished in an instant, and the haze of gray that followed. And looking at Baba now, knowing that she was here to stave off anyone who might tamper with my IV, I remember that darkness can't exist without light.

"It's good to have you back, Thaddeus," Baba says.

A memory surfaces in my mind—the day I saw what Masha did to Shadow, but with a different ending. One where I wasn't afraid to punish her for it. The image is vindicating. I recall the threats she made to me growing up, the implication beneath all of them—*I could kill you, I just choose not to*. But sitting here, staring out the window, I realize I have proof that it was never true. This time, she *did* choose to kill me, and she *couldn't*.

I turn back to Baba, grinning. "It's going to take more than Masha to kill me."

EPILOGUE

I hop into the back of the Uber, setting my faded purple backpack to the side and buckling my seatbelt. My binder is already soaked with sweat from the sweltering Chicago summer, and I readjust it to let some air through. The car's AC is a relief from the humidity, and I sink into my seat, content to enjoy it while it lasts. It's a small pleasure in a day overshadowed by anxiety.

"First day at school?" the driver asks. He's a younger guy, probably only a few years older than me. I check my phone one more time to see what his name is. Viraj. I look at his reflection in the mirror—he has short hair, tapered on the sides, and a shiny black beard which is well kept and flawlessly trimmed. More handsome in person than he looks in his profile picture on the Uber app.

"Yeah," I reply. "And I missed the goddamn bus."

Viraj chuckles. "What time is your class?"

"Ten o'clock."

He glances at his phone, which is mounted on his dashboard. "It's nine thirty. We should get there in time."

I check the route on my phone. It's a twenty minute drive from here to Harry Truman College. "The question is whether I can find my classroom in the remaining ten minutes."

He looks at me through the rear-view mirror. "First time student?"

I bury my anxiety with a chuckle. "Is it that obvious?"

He laughs with me. "Professors usually understand when you're late on your first day," Viraj replies. "You won't be the only person who shows up late because they got lost. It'll be fine, I promise."

He says it with a casual air that I find dumbfounding. School was always hard for me. I could never pay attention to my homework, and had constant clashes with teachers. I had long talks with Matthias about it many times—both of us were kids with mental illness, and instead of the adults in our lives doing anything about it, they just decided not to have faith in either of us. It makes Viraj's carefree attitude all the more frustrating. "I take it you're one of those people who's good at school."

"Hell no," he replies, still retaining his sense of humor. "I've burnt out plenty of times. But as my roommate puts it, C's get degrees."

My irritation fades somewhat. I may not understand his attitude, but the last part of what he says seems true. The conversation fizzles out, and he puts on a true crime podcast to fill the silence. I look over at my backpack, which I've had since middle school. It's heavy, stuffed with my laptop and every accessory that goes with it, along with all the textbooks I need for the day. It's hard to lug the thing around, especially with how quickly I get worn out these days.

The car turns a tight corner, and my stomach lurches. I grimace, then take out my Zofran prescription and pop one in my mouth.

"Motion sickness?" Viraj asks, watching me in the mirror.

"I had surgery on my stomach a little over a year ago," I reply, my voice slurred from the tablet slowly dissolving under my tongue. "Haven't completely recovered just yet."

"Must have been serious."

I sigh heavily. "Yeah, it was pretty gnarly."

Another silence passes. I try to listen to some music on my phone, but when I fumble through my backpack, I can't find my headphones. I groan. First day of college, and I already forgot something important at home. I look out the window, absently watching the buildings go by as I listen to Viraj's podcast.

The advertisement prelude ends, and the intro music plays. The hosts banter a bit, setting a lighthearted tone before getting into their main topic. They say their names—Holly and David—and then jump into the subject matter.

"This one's not as obscure as what we usually cover," Holly says, "but it started a controversy that I think is worth discussing. Plus, getting information on it was easier than I thought it would be."

"Probably because it's so recent," David replies. "Not to mention the political spectacle that followed. A lot of folks were saying it was a hate crime."

"It was," Holly says, already poisoning the well. "Whether it was the intention of the perp isn't clear, but it sparked a lot of national conversation about crimes against minorities that the bigots latched onto. It brought them out of the woodwork, and empowering bigots is the whole point of hate crimes."

A scowl twists my face, and I turn my head away to hide it. I rarely listen to true crime podcasts for this exact reason—there's always some kind of minority at the other end of the gun, and the hosts inevitably sensationalize it. I used to think these podcasts were harmless, but that was before my sister tried to carve out my insides.

"So," David says, "tell me about this case."

"I'm excited for this one," Holly says, with enthusiasm that feels all the more disgusting. "We're going to be talking about the Morozov stabbing."

My heart crashes into my gut. I'm a pipe bomb with a bundle of matches in my throat and a timer I can't see. I thought the hype had died down after more than a year, but apparently the game of telephone surrounding my attempted murder was still ongoing. I have no illusions that this podcast is concerned with accurately representing my story—no one was when it happened, so there's no reason that would have changed now. If these podcast hosts were really interested in the truth, they would have reached out to me. At times I wish I could grab people like these by the shoulders and throttle them, shout at them that *I didn't die! I'm still here!* But that never happens, because that's not the story they want.

After I woke up, I couldn't handle the attention. Every time I heard reporting about my attempted murder, it always painted me as either a helpless victim, a troubled teenager, or an almost-martyr. Depending on what kind of narrative they were selling, it was either a hate crime which was made into a symbol of the horrors the queer community experiences, or a Satanic ritual signaling the end times (a Fox News favorite). My transness is the thing everyone remembers. The fact that I might be a living person with agency never seems to cross their minds.

And that's just my side of the story. The stranger part of all of this was the way people spoke about my sister during the fallout. At best, she was an "interesting case study on psychopathy in women," and at worst people would straight up objectify her. For a while, she became a trending topic on incel forums, whose sexual frustration took her in some really disturbing directions. Inexplicably, people thought she was glamorous—the kind of killer that true crime podcasts like this one love to idolize. My breath becomes harsher as the hosts continue.

"You mentioned that there was some sort of religious ritual involved, according to the reports," David continues, after a poorly-timed ad read for Quip toothbrushes. "What's the real scoop on that?"

"It's actually the first documented case of a Satanic sacrifice," Holly replies, with an annoyingly bubbly tone. "Which makes it a pretty strange intersection of the Sa-

FEVER DREAMS   97

tanic Panic in the '90s, and the Trans Panic of the modern day."

"Oh yeah," David says. I can hear the smile on his voice. "I remember hearing about the Satanism element."

I scoff, then open Discord on my phone. I see that Matthias is online, and I start messaging him.

hellsfavoritenuisance 08/30/2023 9:33 AM

```
bro you will not fuckign believe
this
```

```
my uber driver is listening to a
truecrime podcast about masha
```

mayhematthias 08/30/2023 9:33 AM

```
omg ur famous /j
```

hellsfavoritenuisance 08/30/2023 9:33 AM

```
fuck off lmao
```

```
anyway
```

```
its the usual bullshit about it
being a hate crime
```

mayhematthias 08/30/2023 9:34 AM

```
tbf it did shed some light on crimes
against trans folks
```

```
like im not saying its any less
bullshit obvs
```

```
i just think people dont care about
hate crimes against trans folks as
```

much as they should. any awareness is better than nothing

hellsfavoritenuisance 08/30/2023 9:34 AM
yeah but like

there are real hate crimes out there, being done by real bigots, who are going completely unpunished

masha isnt a transphobe, shes just batshit insane. those 2 things arent mutually inclusive, and the worst transphobes are perfectly level-headed

but reporters love a sensational crime so they paint it that way anyways

mayhematthias 08/30/2023 9:36 AM
along with them claiming its a satanic ritual

bc thats less obscure than russian mythology and makes for better headlines

they keep finding new ways to objectify both of you and its really gross

hellsfavoritenuisance 08/30/2023 9:37 AM

im just tired of people talking
about every trans person as a victim

its part of the reason the suicide
rates are so high

if youre a trans kid and all you see
is news about trans people getting
killed, you might think "i might as
well just kill myself now and save
them the bullet"

why wont they talk about all the
trans people out there who are doing
cool shit

yknow like activists and artists and
researchers and stuff. trans people
who are making the world a better
place

I sigh, watching as we pass a wall covered in graffiti.
It's bright and eye-catching—the kind of outsider art that
everyone disparages, rather than making an effort to ap-
preciate where it comes from. It makes me feel lonely. I
start typing again.

hellsfavoritenuisance 08/30/2023 9:39 AM

everyone talks about trans victims.
no one talks about trans victories

A long pause ensues. Matthias types, erases, then types again.

mayhematthias 08/30/2023 9:41 AM

`co-signed, bc that was some real shit you just said`

`promise me youll tell them that when netflix pitches your biopic`

I chuckle, then check my progress on our route. Halfway to Harry Truman. I put my phone back in my pocket and look out the window again.

"Masha Morozov was really a fascinating case," Holly continues, already painting my sister as the protagonist of this story without an ounce of remorse. "A lot of the same hallmarks of psychopathy that you see with serial killers like Jeffrey Dahmer or Ted Bundy. If she had succeeded, she might have become one herself, making her a rare female serial killer. She would also have been the first one in Chicago ever since Tillie Klimek, over a hundred years ago—at least, as far as we know."

"I guess feminism has come a long way," David jokes. They both laugh. My eye twitches.

"Hey, can you turn that off?" I ask Viraj, narrowly stopping myself from shouting it at him.

"Sure," he says. As he turns down the volume on his bluetooth screen, a shade of recollection passes over his face. He taps on his phone to pause the podcast, then flips back to the Uber app and opens my profile to look at my name and details. His eyebrows fly up, and I hear him curse under his breath. He glances back at me through the mirror. "I'm so sorry."

"It's alright," I lie, swallowing my anger. I stare at my bottle of pills, my stomach churning again. "I can tell you the real story, if you want to hear it."

Viraj nods politely, contemplating my offer for a moment. "If you feel comfortable telling me," he finally replies, "I think I would like to know."

He speaks in a way that's refreshingly earnest. Not a reporter trying to put a spin on it, not a lawyer trying to build a case. Unlike most people I spoke to after the fact, he hasn't already made up his mind about it. Just a regular guy who wants to hear the truth. I nod, smile, and begin my story. "Well, for one thing, Masha isn't a Satanist."

ABOUT THE AUTHOR

Dev Solovey is a queer, dis-
abled artist who has been telling
stories since childhood. Drawing on his work in behavioral
health as well as personal experi-
ence, his writing often uses unexpected premises to explore
the human experience, overcoming trauma and bias, mental illness and addiction, and the vibrancy of mortality.

His current projects include the low-fantasy webcomic
Devil Went Down to Vegas, short stories on Royal Road,
and Dread-libs, a horror-comedy podcast hosted by Unveiling Nightmares. He is a native of Tucson, Arizona.

You can find links to his projects on his link-
tree: https://linktr.ee/devsolovey

Made in the USA
Columbia, SC
15 August 2024

40054778R00061